AMADON

ALERT

Paul Davies

Oxford University Press

It was a hot afternoon in Vila Nova. It was too hot.

'There's nothing to do,' Lucia said. 'Nothing exciting happens here.'

'I know,' said Pedro. 'This town is too quiet.'

Suddenly, Rosanna saw a boat on the river.

'Hmm,' she said. 'Very strange.'

'What's the matter?' Pedro asked.

'Well, that boat is moving,' Rosanna answered. 'But there's nobody in it.'

Lucia stood up. 'I'm going to tell my father. Something's wrong.'

Lucia ran home and found her father.

'Come quickly!' she said.

Her father didn't open his eyes. 'I'm sleeping,' he said.

'No you're not,' said Lucia. 'Please come with me. I think it's important.'

Lucia's father slowly got up. 'All right,' he said, tiredly.

Lucia and her father went back to the river. He looked at the boat and he thought for a few seconds.

'It's very strange,' he said. 'I don't understand.'

Some more people arrived. They all looked at the strange boat. Nobody could understand.

'Wait!' Lucia said, suddenly. 'Look carefully. There *is* something – or somebody – in the boat.'

'How do you know that?' Pedro and Rosanna asked.

- How does Lucia know?

'Look at the water,' said Lucia. 'That boat is more in the water than the other boats.'

'Yes, very good,' Lucia's father said. 'I saw that too.'

When they looked in the boat, they found a man.

'Don't look,' Lucia's father said to the children. 'He's . . . he's dead.'

'Urgh! And his face is yellow,' Lucia said, moving nearer.

'Who is he?' Rosanna asked.

'He's not from this town,' a woman said. 'I don't know him.'

'He was a botanist,' Lucia's father said. 'He arrived here last week. He wanted to study the flowers in the forest.'

'Come on,' a man said. 'We must go to his house. Perhaps we can find something there.'

'Look at all these books!' said Pedro, when they were in the botanist's house. 'There are thousands of them!'

'And maps,' said Lucia.

'And these letters,' said Rosanna.

'Letters?' Lucia said. 'That's interesting. Can you read them?'

'Er . . . no, I can't.' Rosanna answered. 'Look. It's a very strange language.'

'Does this help?' Pedro asked. He gave Rosanna a book.

- Can you read the letter?

'I think I can read it,' Lucia said, slowly. 'It says: "Today I found a new flower in the forest. I'm going to be famous at last!"'

'So what happened?' Pedro asked.

'I don't know,' Lucia's father answered.

Just then, they heard a noise. A man ran into the botanist's house.

'Quickly!' he said. 'Quickly, come with me. There's another boat. And another body!'

'I don't like this,' Pedro said.

They all went back to the river, and saw the body. Again, the face was yellow. But now there was a stranger next to the body.

'I saw everything,' the stranger said. 'You must all leave this town. You're all going to die.'

'What happened?' a man asked.

'I was at Santa Cruz,' the stranger answered. 'Your friend was in his boat. Suddenly, yellow smoke came out of the water. The smoke killed him. It all happened very quickly. I couldn't help him.'

At first, nobody spoke. Then a woman said 'He's right! We must leave. It's too dangerous here.'

But Rosanna remembered the map in the botanist's house. 'The stranger's story isn't true,' she thought.

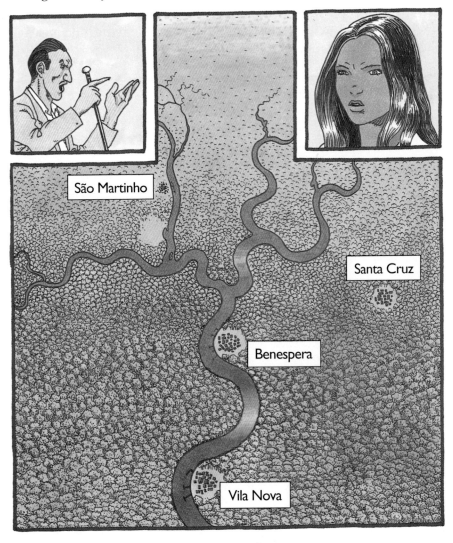

- How does Rosanna know that the stranger's story isn't true? Look at the map.

They went back to the botanist's house and Rosanna showed them the map.

'The stranger's story can't be true,' Rosanna said. 'Look. He said that he was in Santa Cruz. But Santa Cruz isn't near the river!'

'You're right,' Lucia said. 'We must tell everybody.'

'It's too late,' Lucia's father said. 'People are leaving Vila Nova. They say it's too dangerous here. They're afraid.'

Lucia thought for a few minutes. 'What happened to the botanist?' she said. 'Where did he go? How did he die?'

'Perhaps this can tell us,' Pedro said. 'Look. It's another letter.'

'Give it to me,' Lucia said. 'Hmm. This is what it says ...'

Yesterday I found a new flower. Today I'm going back there, because I want to look for more. I need to go up the river, past Benespera. Then I go left, and then right. I go past a clearing on the left, and then I'm there!

'That doesn't help,' Pedro said. 'What was the place called?'

'It *does* help,' Rosanna said. 'We can look at the map again! Then we can see where he went.'

- Look at the letter and look at the map on page 7.
  Where did the botanist find the flower?

'Look. He went to São Martinho,' Rosanna said.

'And I'm going to go there tonight,' Lucia said. 'But don't tell my father.'

'I'm going to go with you,' Rosanna said. 'Pedro?'

Pedro looked afraid. 'Isn't it too dangerous?'

'You don't need to come,' Lucia said.

'No, wait,' Pedro said. 'I want to go too.'

'We can take my father's boat,' Lucia said. 'Meet me by the river tonight.'

At midnight the forest was very dark. They couldn't see anything, but they could hear a lot of strange noises.

'Where are we?' Lucia asked.

'I think we're near São Martinho,' Pedro answered.

'Be quiet!' Rosanna said suddenly. 'What's that noise?'

They all listened carefully.

'There are people in the forest,' Lucia said. 'Men. And they're very near us, too. Let's go and look.'

The three friends left the boat. Soon they found a clearing.

'Look!' Pedro said. 'They're destroying the forest.'

'We must stop them,' Rosanna said.

'No. We must go and tell my father first,' said Lucia. 'Perhaps he can stop them.'

'But is he going to believe us?' Rosanna asked.

'I don't know,' Lucia answered. 'Why don't we take those keys? Then he must believe us.'

- How can they get the keys?

This is how they took the keys

'Quickly! Back to the boat!' said Rosanna.

But when they arrived at the boat, they saw the stranger.

'Ah, there you are!' he said. 'Come here.'

'Run!' said Pedro, and they ran back into the forest.

'Where do we go?' asked Lucia.

'I don't know,' Rosanna answered. 'But don't stop running! The stranger's getting closer.'

'Where are we?' asked Pedro. 'It's too dark. I can't see.'

They ran through the forest.

'I want to go home,' said Pedro. 'I'm afraid.'

'We all want to go home,' Rosanna said. 'But we don't know where we are. It's too dark, and the forest is too big.'

'There's a clearing!' Lucia said.

'And there's another one,' Rosanna said.

'There are four clearings,' Pedro said. 'But look! There are snakes too!'

'Are they dangerous?' asked Rosanna.

'Some snakes are dangerous,' Pedro answered. 'But which ones?'

- All black snakes are dangerous.
- Yellow snakes are not dangerous.
- Big green snakes are dangerous but little green snakes are not dangerous.

- Which clearing can they go through?

'Quickly!' said Lucia. 'The clearing on the left. Come on!'

'Urgh! I hate snakes!' Pedro said.

'Forget the snakes,' said Lucia. 'And don't stop running. I can see the river. And some boats!'

'Where's the stranger?' Rosanna asked. 'I think I can hear him.'

'So can I,' said Pedro. 'He isn't very far away.'

'We need a boat,' said Rosanna. 'Look! Here comes the stranger. He's going to see us. Quickly!'

'But there are lots of boats here,' Pedro said. 'Which one is our boat?'

'It doesn't matter,' Rosanna answered.

'It *does* matter,' said Lucia. 'We need to have the key, or we can't start the boat.'

'Aren't those the keys for a boat?' Pedro asked.

'Hmm. Yes, I think so,' Rosanna said. 'But which boat?'

'Well, think!' Lucia said. 'Do you remember that man? He was asleep, remember? And we could see his shoes.'

'Yes!' said Pedro, suddenly. 'And look at the ground!'

- Which boat do they need? Look carefully at the picture on page 11.

'It's the blue boat,' said Pedro. 'Oh no! Here's the stranger. Quick, run!'

Rosanna, Lucia and Pedro ran to the blue boat and got in.

'Start the boat,' Lucia said.

They started the boat and began to move down the river.

'At last!' said Pedro. 'We can go home now.'

'Can we?' Rosanna said. 'We don't know where we are, remember? And look! The stranger's got a boat too. Faster, Pedro!'

'All right, all right,' Pedro said. 'But where?'

'It doesn't matter,' Lucia said. 'Just go faster!'

They went faster, but the stranger went faster too.

'I think his boat is better,' Lucia said.

Just then, the stranger stopped his boat. He looked at the three children in their boat, and he smiled.

'Why is he smiling?' Rosanna asked. 'And why isn't he moving?'

'I don't know,' Lucia answered. 'But don't stop the boat.'

'Hmm,' Pedro thought. 'Perhaps he knows something . . .'

'Stop the boat! Stop the boat!' said Lucia, suddenly. 'Look! We can't go through there!'

'I can't stop the boat,' said Pedro. 'The river's moving too fast.'

'Be careful, Pedro!' said Rosanna.

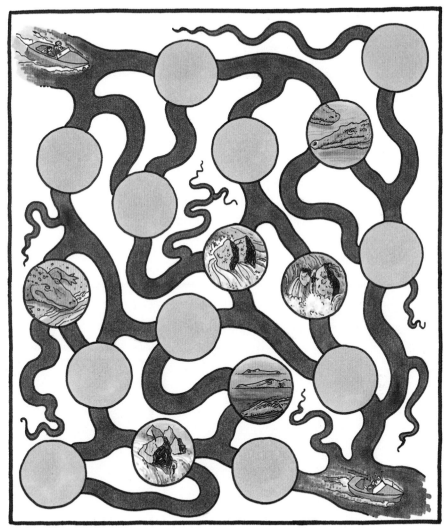

- Tell Pedro where to go. You can only go on green circles. Don't go on circles where there are rocks or alligators.

'I don't believe it!' Rosanna said. 'We're alive.'

'Yes, but where are we?' asked Lucia. 'And where's Vila Nova?'

'I don't know,' Pedro answered, 'but I can see a village. Perhaps we can ask there.'

Lucia, Pedro and Rosanna left the boat and went to the village. They found some houses, but nobody was there.

'Why did everybody leave?' asked Pedro.

'I don't know,' Lucia answered. 'Perhaps they left because of the stranger and the men in the forest.'

'Look at that!' Rosanna said, suddenly. 'It's a temple.'
'It's thousands of years old,' said Lucia. 'Shall we go inside?'
'Why?' asked Pedro.
'Because it's exciting,' Lucia answered. 'Come on.'
'I don't like this,' Pedro said. 'I want to go back to Vila Nova.'
They went inside. Suddenly, the door closed behind them.
'I told you!' said Pedro. 'How are we going to get out now?'

- How can they get out of the temple?

'It's very dark in here,' said Lucia.

'It's cold, too,' said Pedro. 'And what's that strange noise?'

Rosanna listened. 'Hmm. Snakes, I think.'

'Snakes?' said Pedro. 'Quick! Let's find another door.'

They walked slowly through the old temple. It was difficult to see. There were spiders and insects, as well as snakes. Pedro was afraid.

'I don't understand why Lucia wanted to come in here,' he thought.

'There *must* be another door,' said Lucia, 'and we're going to find it.'

'When Lucia wants to do something, nothing can stop her,' thought Pedro.

After a long time, they found the door.

'At last! Now can we go back to Vila Nova?' asked Pedro.

'All right,' Lucia said. 'We have to tell my father about those men in the forest.'

They went back to the boat.

'I know this place!' Rosanna said, suddenly. 'My father's friend lives in that house. We aren't far from Vila Nova.'

When they got back, they went to see Lucia's father.

'You must come with us,' Lucia said. 'There are some men – they're destroying the forest! We must stop them. And the stranger! He's dangerous. He wanted to kill us! And …'

'Sit down,' Lucia's father said. 'And tell me everything – slowly!'

Lucia told her father everything.

'We must stop them,' he said at last. 'I'm going to call the police. Then you can take us to this place in the forest.'

When the police arrived, they all went to look for the men in the forest. But the men weren't there.

'They were here yesterday,' Rosanna said. 'I know they were here.'

Lucia looked at her father. Then she looked at the forest.

'We're too late,' she said, 'this time. But next time, I'm going to stop them.'

- Look at the picture. Can you see something that belongs to the stranger?

Glossary

alligator a large, long animal that lives in rivers in hot countries; it has a lot of teeth and is very dangerous

believe if you **believe** someone, you think that what they are saying is right

boat people go across rivers or the sea in **boats**

botanist someone who is very interested in flowers

clearing a place where there are no trees, in the middle of a forest

destroy to kill

forest a place with lots of trees

key a small thing used to open and shut doors

snake a long thin animal with no legs; some snakes are dangerous

stranger someone you do not know

study (v) to learn everything you can about something

temple a very old building

walking stick a long thin piece of wood; people sometimes hold a **walking stick** when they go walking

Answers to the puzzles

page 5
Today I found a new flower in the forest. I'm going to be famous at last!

page 7
The stranger says that he found the dead man in a boat in Santa Cruz. Rosanna knows that there is no river at Santa Cruz.

page 9
Look at the map on page 7. Begin at Vila Nova and go up the river. Turn left at Benespera, then turn right. Go past the clearing on the left and you come to São Martinho.

page 13
The clearing near Lucia, at the top on the left.

page 15
They can see the marks of the guard's shoes on the ground, near the blue boat, so they know that his key must be the key for the blue boat.

page 21
The stranger's walking stick is next to the tree.

Oxford University Press, Great Clarendon Street, Oxford OX2 6DP

Oxford   New York
Athens Auckland Bangkok Bogotá Buenos Aires Cape Town
Chennai Dar es Salaam Delhi Florence Hong Kong Istanbul Karachi
Kolkata Kuala Lumpur Madrid Melbourne Mexico City Mumbai Nairobi
Paris São Paulo Shanghai Singapore Taipei Tokyo Toronto Warsaw

with associated companies in Berlin   Ibadan

OXFORD and OXFORD ENGLISH are trade marks
of Oxford University Press

ISBN 0 19 422485 6

© Oxford University Press 1994

First published 1994
Ninth impression 2001

No unauthorized photocopying

Illustrated by Rob Taylor

Typeset by Tradespools Ltd., Frome, Somerset

Printed in Hong Kong